GRIZZLY BEARS & BEAVER PELTS

Book 1 – Tuff, Sadie & The Wild West
Book 2 – General Muster & No-Trees Town
Book 3 – Grizzly Bears & Beaver Pelts

Coming soon:

Book 4 – Macho Nacho & The Cowboy Battle
Book 5 – The Parrot Gang & Wild West Ghosts
Book 6 – The Nasty Boys & The Bobbies

To Vy,

GRIZZLY BEARS & BEAVER PELTS

Hideout Kids Book 3

Mike Gleason

by Mike Gleason

Illustrated by Victoria Taylor

FARM STREET PUBLISHING

First published 2017 by Farm Street Publishing
www.hideoutkidsbooks.com

Paperback ISBN 978-1-912207-06-0
Hardback ISBN 978-1-912207-07-7
eBook ISBN 978-1-912207-08-4

A CIP catalogue record for this book is available from
the British Library.

Design and typesetting by Head & Heart
Printed and bound by Lightning Source

To Michelle and Luke,
who inspired me to write these stories
of the Wild West.

TUFF

SADIE

WILD THING

CONTENTS

Dear Reader,

Grizzly Bears & Beaver Pelts is the third in the series of Hideout Kids books.

In the early days of the Wild West a few explorers set out to trap beavers. Beaver furs, known as "pelts", were made into hats. Beaver hats were very popular all over the world, so the pelts were as valuable as bars of gold. Since many of the beavers built their dams across streams in the Rocky Mountains, the beaver trappers became known as "Mountain Men". The pelts didn't just attract tough Mountain Men, who lived in rough conditions in the wilderness. Outlaws often attacked the Mountain Men and tried to steal their beaver pelts.

In this story, the powerful and good witch Judge June Beak sends Sheriff Tuff and Deputy Sadie back in time to rescue the most famous Mountain Man of all, Jedediah Smith, from a gang of vicious outlaws. The outlaws are trying to steal his valuable beaver pelts, as he makes his way across the dangerous Rocky Mountains.

If you want to curl up with a good story, start curling and turn the page.

Mike Gleason

Black Hills

Rocky Mountains

South Pass

Bighorn River

WYOMING
TERRITORY

HONEY HONEY HONEY

April 1871

TUFF AND SADIE'S
JOURNEY TO HELP
JEDEDIAH SMITH

Muleshoe

The Cave

TEXAS

GRIZZLY BEARS & BEAVER PELTS

CHAPTER ONE

APRIL FOOLS

It was a warm spring afternoon in the Wild West Texas town of Muleshoe.

Sheriff Tuff Brunson nodded off in his rocking chair. He had just finished a delicious lunch of tacos and burritos.

As Tuff fell asleep, he heard the tiny cowboy poet singing. The song drifted in through the jailhouse window:

Chief Black Bear's gang
Trapped a Mountain Man
Though the gang was small
They had a great plan

'Cause the giant Mountain Men
Have just one scare
They fear nothing in the world
'Cept a giant grizzly bear

Just behind Tuff, locked inside a cell, was the meanest outlaw in the Wild West, "Big Nose" George Parrot. Big Nose George was sound asleep too.

"BAM!" "SLAM!" "KERPOW!" came a pounding on the door to the jailhouse.

"What the –?" Tuff said as his eyes struggled open.

"What made that noise?" he said to Deputy Dan, his assistant jailer. "Open the door and let's have a look."

Deputy Dan let out a loud "SNORE!" and stayed fast asleep in his own rocking chair. Deputy Dan always ate twice as many tacos and burritos as Tuff. His snore was soon followed by a loud "BURP!"

Amazing. He even burps in his sleep, thought Tuff.

"You're impossible to wake up," Tuff said to Deputy Dan. "Sadie!" he yelled.

Deputy Sadie Marcus ran into the room from her jailhouse office.

"Did you hear that noise?" Tuff asked her.

"Of course I did," said Sadie. "Someone, or something, was pounding on the door. Let's have a look outside and see what's going on."

"Is your bullwhip ready?" Tuff asked.

"Yep," Sadie said as her fingers curled around the handle of her whip.

Tuff checked the leather bullwhip hanging from his belt before he carefully cracked the door open. He and Sadie peeped outside.

"Good afternoon," said a voice from somewhere near the door. "Would you like to buy some cakes today?"

"No, we don't want any cakes," Tuff said, looking around.

"Then how about some candies?" said the voice.

"No candies either," said Tuff, still trying to see who was talking.

"Ice cream?" said the voice.

"No," said Tuff.

"Would you like to see who this is?" said the voice. "Step outside; it's a surprise."

Tuff whispered to Sadie, "Hey, today is the first of April. I think it's Jelly Roll Jim. He's playing an April Fools' joke on us. Let's play along and go out."

The two law officers stepped outside the door.

"Ha, ha, you're trapped," said the voice as a rope net came down on them from above. They struggled to break free but they couldn't move.

"You thought this was April Fools' but the joke's on you," shouted "Little Nose" George Parrot, Big Nose George's younger brother.

"Yeah Sheriff," squeaked "Tiny Nose"

Peggy Parrot, the youngest member of the outlaw Parrot Gang. "Nah, nah, ha, ha, Happy April Fools' Day, 'cept we're not your friends and we don't care if you're happy."

"Listen, you pretty Parrots," said Tuff. "Get this net off us right now or you'll spend the rest of your lives eating bird food, locked up inside the jail with your smelly brother."

"We'll see who's gonna be locked up, Sheriff," said Little Nose George. "Peggy, grab the keys off Deputy Dan and let's do a jail cell switcheroo. Big Nose George out, the two Dep-u-ties in."

"Wake up, Deputy Dan," Tuff yelled. "We need your help."

"SNORE!" came the reply from Deputy Dan's rocking chair. "BURP!"

Peggy and Little Nose George headed into the jailhouse.

"I don't know, Sadie," Tuff said. "Even an explosion couldn't wake up Deputy Dan!"

Wait. Explosion. Tuff remembered something very important. He smiled to himself.

"Hang on, Little Nose Peggy-Bird brain," Tuff said. "Deputy Dan doesn't have the keys. They're in my desk drawer."

Tuff grinned as Tiny Nose Peggy and Little Nose George jumped over to the desk and yanked the drawer open.

"POP!" A booby trap exploded, spraying sleeping gas in the two outlaws' faces. They quickly fell to the ground, fast asleep from the gas.

"What the –?" said Deputy Dan as he leapt out of his chair. "Tuff, why are you and Sadie wrapped up in a net?" he asked, rubbing his eyes.

"You were wrong, Tuff." Sadie smiled. "An explosion *did* wake up Deputy Dan."

"Get this net off us, Deputy Dan," Tuff said. "Let's tie up those two clipped Parrots before they fly around causing more of a ruckus."

CHAPTER TWO

JUDGE JUNE HAS AN URGENT JOB

Tuff locked the Parrots in the jail cell with their brother then grabbed the net Little Nose George had thrown around him and Sadie.

"Here you go, ugly Parrot Gang," he said as he tossed the net into the cell. "Maybe you can catch a few mosquitoes flying around the cell. For your supper."

"So you got us this time, Sheriff Brunson," growled Big Nose George. The explosion had woken him too. "But we'll all be out agin before you can say sarsaparilla."

"Oh, go blow your snoot, Big Nose. Your nose is so big you'll make a snot river, where you can go swimming," Tuff said as he put on his white hat and looked at Sadie. "That Parrot Gang is the worst excuse for an outlaw gang I've ever seen. They're like parrot chicks."

"Yeah, they're always up to their teenage tricks. Let's go get a nice cold sarsaparilla at the saloon," Sadie said. "Judge June should be there. I bet she has a job for us."

"You're in charge of the jail, Deputy Dan," Tuff said over his shoulder as he and Sadie left the jailhouse and went out into Muleshoe's dusty main road. "Try to stay awake."

Tuff's broad white hat shaded his head from the sun, while his belt with golden stars sparkled in the daylight.

"Wonder if I'll get a star from Judge June for jailing those two Parrots?" Tuff said. "Judge June gives me a golden star every time I catch an outlaw."

"You might," said Sadie. "When you fill the belt you'll be a United States Marshall, top lawman in the Wild West."

The Deputies walked into the rowdy Happy Days Saloon, where they spotted Judge Junia "June" Beak chatting with Toothless Tom, the bartender.

The saloon smelled of hot chocolate and yummy s'mores as the Muleshoe hideout kids gobbled their afternoon snacks.

"Howdy Tuff, howdy Sadie," said Judge

June as they came up to her. "I'd love to share a s'more but we've got a very urgent job to discuss. Let's go over to my hut where it's quiet."

Tuff glanced at Sadie as they followed Judge June out of the saloon. "This must be a serious job," he said. "Judge June loves her s'mores."

"I love mine, too, especially with a cold sarsaparilla," said Sadie. Her black ponytails bounced on her shoulders as they walked through the yellow door into Judge June's hut.

Tuff felt its cool, magical air surround him as she closed the door behind them.

CHAPTER THREE

A JOB IN THE OLD WEST

The hut was more of a mess than usual, with books and maps strewn all over Judge June's desk. The calendar on the wall was marked with the date, April 1st.

In the corner stood a black bear with gnashing teeth and long sharp claws.

So glad the bear is dead and stuffed. Tuff shivered. *Are his eyes following me?*

"Thanks for wakin' me up," growled Wild Thing, Judge June's pet pink fairy armadillo.

"If you wake me, you feed me. That's the deal. Where's my mash?"

"Right here, honeybunch," Sadie said as she put a bowl of ground-up black widow spiders and tarantulas in front of Wild Thing.

"I don't want tarantulas today," Wild Thing shouted. "Got any head lice?"

"Sure, here you go," Sadie said. "I found these on Deputy Dan."

Judge June said, "I send you to fight villains all over the Wild West. For this job, you have to journey back through time."

"How will we do that?" Sadie asked. "Using magic?"

"Yes," said Judge June. "But for this magic to work you have to go to a special place – The Cave. There's a secret path behind the stables that'll take you there. Spiky the Cactus guards the entrance and will show you what to do."

"Will we have Silver Heels and Jenny?" Tuff joined in. The Deputies loved Tuff's muscled chestnut colt Silver Heels and his sister, the rugged black mare Jenny, who Sadie rode.

"BURP!" went Wild Thing.

"Please, Wild Thing, have some manners," Judge June scolded. "Yes, you'll need your horses. You'll travel back to the year 1830 to join an expedition led by Jedediah Smith."

"The famous Old West explorer and beaver trapper," Tuff said. "I read about him in the history section of *This Week in the Wild West*. He started The Rendezvous, which was the name he gave to a big party for all his explorer friends."

"Exactly," said Judge June. "Jedediah Smith is leading a team of twelve explorers through the Black Hills near the Rocky Mountains. They're pinned down at a campsite by an outlaw Sioux Tribe Indian gang. He has one week to reach South Pass of the Bighorn River in Wyoming territory. If he doesn't make it, winter will set in and the chance will be lost."

"Winter in the Rocky Mountains is hard,"

said Sadie. "I heard the snow drifts get as high as tall trees."

"Your job is to get the outlaw gang away from Jedediah. If the team can make it to the Bighorn River a new exploration route to the West will be opened," said Judge June. "If you don't manage to help him, history will be changed. America might stop at the Mississippi River."

Tuff fingered his bullwhip. "I'm ready." He hoped he'd be lucky with it again – he always seemed to hit his targets but he wasn't sure how it happened.

"Any more questions?" asked Judge June.

"I'm worried about The Cave," Tuff said. "What if we get sent to the wrong year?"

"Don't worry, Tuff," Judge June said with a calm smile. "That won't happen."

"Should we worry about anything besides the winter and the outlaws?" Sadie asked.

"You won't have to worry about winter itself," said Judge June. "But you might need to be careful of something much more dangerous. The giant grizzly bears are preparing to hibernate so they eat everything they can find. You'll be going into the heart of grizzly country."

"I'm sure our bullwhips can handle any ole grizzly bear," Tuff said shakily, as he glanced at the stuffed bear in the corner.

"Let me go," Wild Thing yelled. "They're probably scared of bears. I eat grizzlies for breakfast. Grr... Grr..."

"Yeah, right, Wild Thing." Judge June laughed. "Maybe your bad breath could chase them off. You can get bad breath from talking too much."

"Blah, blah, blah," Wild Thing growled as she rolled over on her back and fell asleep.

"I'll give you something to help with the bears," Judge June said to Tuff and Sadie. "Both of you close your eyes tightly. Stay completely silent." She raised her arms and chanted a few words as she cast a spell over

her brave sheriff and deputy.

"Open your eyes now," said Judge June.

Tuff and Sadie looked up into the gaze of the magical Judge June's blue-gray almond-shaped eyes.

"Be at The Cave at first light tomorrow morning," she said. "When you get there, Spiky the Cactus will ask you for the password. It's 'Jedediah'."

Tuff and Sadie turned to go. "And remember," added Judge June, "it's easier to *stay* out of trouble than to *get* out of trouble. Be careful."

CHAPTER FOUR

INTO THE CAVE

The next morning Tuff and Sadie woke to the songs of mockingbirds and red cardinals.

"Let's get out to the stables and saddle up the horses," Tuff said after a big yawn. "Man, I slept badly last night. I kept thinking about grizzly bears."

"Don't worry about the bears," said Sadie as she braided her straight black hair. "Our bullwhips can keep them well away from us."

They put on their law-officer outfits, fitted their hats, then grabbed their saddlebags and headed for the stables.

"What are you putting in there?" Tuff asked as Sadie wrapped up jars and stuffed them into her saddlebags. "Those look like the jars Toothless Tom keeps behind his bar. Did you tell him you took them?"

"Um, no. But it's just a few jars of bees' honey," she said. "You know how much I like it on my porridge in the morning. We never seem to find any honey out on the trails. Toothless Tom won't even know they're gone."

"Yes, he will, Sadie. You have to stop taking things from people without their permission," Tuff scolded. "Anyway, did you remember the sugar water for the bullwhips? The whips stay flexible if we dip them in sugar water each night."

"It's right here," Sadie said, "but maybe you should worry a bit more about the scorpion crawling toward you than what I'm putting in my saddlebags, Sheriff Tuff."

Tuff turned and hollered as he saw a striped bark scorpion slither under his boots.

"What the –?" said Tuff. "Look out. One bite from him and we'll be toast."

"NEIGH!"

Tuff and Sadie leapt up on the stable fence as Sadie's big black mare Jenny stomped and snorted at the scorpion. It turned and ran under a pile of hay.

"Good girl," said Sadie as she patted Jenny's nose. "Here's a nice candied apple. Thanks for looking after the sheriff."

"You're welcome," Jenny neighed.

Tuff and Sadie hopped up on Silver Heels and Jenny. They guided their horses out of the stables along the secret path to The Cave.

"What else do you know about Jedediah Smith?" Sadie asked as she tucked her boots into her stirrups.

Tuff replied, "The fur trappers and explorers were called 'Mountain Men'. They

were very brave. Jedediah Smith was as huge as a giant and not afraid of anything. He was known as 'The King of the Mountain Men'."

They rode up Bear's Ears Canyon, through pastures full of blooming bluebonnets. At the top of the canyon, hidden behind Boiling Springs, they found a cave.

Beside the entrance was a huge saguaro cactus covered in long, sharp needles.

"Look, that must be Spiky," Tuff whispered. "He's as high as the sky."

Tuff walked Silver Heels slowly up to the fierce-looking cactus.

"Howdy, Spiky," Tuff said as he stared up at the giant cactus.

"Hello, Spiky," Sadie added. She was right behind Tuff, on Jenny.

"Howdy," answered Spiky, "You must be Sheriff Tuff Brunson and Deputy Sadie Marcus. I hear you'd like to visit some beaver trappers. Got the password?"

"Jedediah," said Tuff.

"Enter The Cave. When you're ready, say 'let's go', and away you'll go."

Tuff and Sadie rode into The Cave. It was pitch black and not a sound could be heard.

"Ready, Sadie?" Tuff could hardly see her in the gloom.

"Yep. Let's hope this works."

"Alright then," said Tuff nervously. "Let's go."

They closed their eyes as a low rumble and a cool breeze filled The Cave.

When the rumble stopped, Tuff and Sadie opened their eyes. Before them was a dark green forest. Mountains with snowy peaks rose in the distance. They shivered a bit as the cold winter air greeted them.

Silver Heels' ears pricked up as Tuff spurred him slowly forward out of The Cave and toward the forest. *Does he sense trouble already?*

"Sadie, stay close," he said. "I'm not sure what to expect."

"You can expect to tell me what you're doing here," growled a voice. "You and your sidekick can get down off those horses."

CHAPTER FIVE

TUFF & SADIE MEET THE MOUNTAIN MEN

Tuff looked straight ahead, right down the barrel of a rifle.

"Who are you?" Tuff said.

"I'm a Mountain Man. Name's Tom Fitzpatrick but everybody calls me Broken Hand," the owner of the rifle said as he pointed it at Tuff. "This is my posse." He nodded at the ten Mountain Men around him. "Get off those horses. Now," he said.

Tuff decided not to argue. *Broken Hand is as big as a bear,* he thought. Sadie dismounted too.

"What are you doing here? Little kids shouldn't be ridin' around up here," said Broken Hand, as he grabbed the reins of the horses and handed them to one of his Mountain Men.

"I'm Sheriff Tuff Brunson," Tuff answered. "This is Deputy Sadie Marcus. We've been sent to help Jedediah Smith fight off the outlaw Sioux Tribe gang which has him and his team trapped at a campsite."

"Sheriff and Deputy? You're just children. Who sent you?" asked Broken Hand.

"We were sent by Judge Junia Beak," said Tuff as he glanced at Sadie.

"I've never heard of Judge Junia Beak or you, either," said Broken Hand, as he lowered his rifle and extended his good hand to Tuff. "I don't know where you come from. But if you're here to help Jedediah I'm glad to see you. I'm Jedediah Smith's Wagon Boss."

"Whew, glad to meet you," smiled Tuff shaking Tom's hand. "Please shake hands with Sadie."

"Howdy, Sadie," said Broken Hand. "Welcome to –"

"THWACK!" An arrow whooshed over Broken Hand's head and stuck into a tree just behind him. "THWACK!" Another followed it.

"Get down," hollered Broken Hand. "It's an ambush. It must be the outlaws."

Broken Hand and his posse formed a ring around Tuff, Sadie and the horses. Tuff and Sadie grabbed their bullwhips.

"Look out, you dirty outlaws," cried Tuff. "Here comes Sheriff Tuff Brunson!" "CRACK!"

"Here comes Deputy Sadie!" yelled Sadie. "CRACK!"

The Deputies' whips flew through the air and snapped around the bows of the outlaws.

As the whips coiled up they yanked the bows out of the outlaws' hands.

Tuff saw two shadows moving away through the forest.

"Wow," said Broken Hand. "I've never seen bullwhips as fast as yours. It's like magic."

"Who were they?" Tuff said as he winked at Sadie, knowing that whether the whips were magical or not somehow Judge June's spell was helping them.

"They call themselves the Black Arrow Gang," Broken Hand said. "Their leader is Chief Black Bear. They use arrows to keep us pinned down; they don't have any guns. It looks like they've left for now. Let's ride over to meet Jedediah. Stay close behind us. You're just kids. I don't want you getting lost."

Tuff and Sadie hopped back on Silver Heels and Jenny and followed the Mountain Men deeper into the forest.

"Broken Hand is huge," whispered Sadie to Tuff.

"Do you think he's almost as big as a bear?" said Tuff. "'Cause I do."

"Bigger," said Sadie. "Look, here's their campsite."

"It sure smells funny around here," Tuff said as they rode into the camp. "And I think I know why."

"That smell is dried-up buffalo poop," Broken Hand said. "We burn it to keep warm, also to cook our food."

Tuff laughed, "Bet that makes the food taste dee-lish!"

"Yuk!" Sadie held her nose as they rode up to a tent in the middle of the camp. "This tent looks like a whole army could live in it," she said.

"A whole army does live in it," said Broken Hand quietly as he looked at the open flap of the tent. "A one-man army named Jedediah Smith."

Out of the tent walked the biggest giant of a man Tuff had ever seen. As the giant strode

toward them the ground shook, like there was an earthquake.

"What did you find here, Broken Hand?" roared Jedediah Smith as he looked down at Tuff and Sadie. "Did you go out looking for tiny elves in the forest?"

Although Tuff was sitting on Silver Heels he still had to look up at Jedediah Smith.

"Hello, Jedediah," Tuff said as he pushed his white hat back on his head then puffed out his chest. "I'm Sheriff Tuff Brunson and this is Deputy Sadie Marcus. We've been sent by Judge Junia Beak to help you fight the Black Arrow Gang. We intend to send them on their way so you can continue your trip to the Bighorn River."

"Send them on their way, did you say?" bellowed Jedediah Smith. "Good luck. They've had us pinned down for a week. They want to steal our beaver pelts. You little elves don't have guns or bows and arrows. All you have are those bullwhips. Chief Black Bear will be laughing when he sees you. Kids can't fight him."

"He won't be laughing if he sees them use those whips, Jedediah," said Broken Hand. "They're faster than their own shadows. I've never seen anything like it."

"Oh, nonsense," said Jedediah. "They're no help. If we don't get out soon we'll never get to South Pass before winter."

Sadie reached down and felt her bullwhip. "I don't think Chief Black Bear will be laughing at us, Mr. Smith. Crime doesn't pay."

"Neither do I," said Tuff, as he stared straight ahead. "We'll see who's laughing."

CHAPTER SIX

TUFF HAS A PLAN

"Alright then, come sit by the campfire," said Jedediah Smith. "We've got plenty of buffalo chips to burn. They'll keep us warm while I tell you about Chief Black Bear."

Tuff, Sadie and Broken Hand joined Jedediah Smith around the campfire.

"Chief Black Bear comes from over yonder Black Hills," said Jedediah Smith. "He was a member of the Sioux Tribe but they got scared of him and his pets and threw him out."

"His pets?" asked Tuff. "You mean dogs and cats? What's so scary about them?"

"No, I mean pet *grizzly bears*," said Jedediah Smith. "He's got two of them. They're big and hungry."

"Oh dear," said Tuff.

"You can say that again," said Sadie.

"Oh dear," said Tuff.

"OK, enough 'Oh dears'," said Jedediah Smith. "Chief Black Bear took the meanest outlaw Sioux Indians he could find then formed the Black Arrow Gang. They've been stealing beaver pelts from our trapper and explorer friends. They use their bows and arrows. They can shoot an apple right off the top of your head."

"What about their pet grizzlies?" Tuff asked. "Do they keep them in cages?"

"Cages?" answered Broken Hand. "Ha. The bears roam free. They've been with Chief Black Bear since they were little cubs. The grizzlies think Chief Black Bear is their mother."

"How many outlaws are in the Black Arrow Gang?" asked Tuff.

"There are only six of them," said Jedediah Smith. "Plus the two bears."

"Jedediah," said Tuff. "Why don't you just fight the gang? You have more trappers. Also, I heard you aren't afraid of anything."

"Well, Tuff," said Jedediah Smith. "You're right. I'm not afraid of anything *human*."

"Oh. I understand now."

"Yep," said Jedediah Smith. "I'm scared to death of grizzly bears."

"Me too," said Broken Hand.

"We too," shouted all the Mountain Men.

"So are we," whinnied their horses.

"I have an idea," said Tuff. "They don't know who Sadie and I are. We can disguise ourselves as Sioux Tribe Indians and join their gang. Once they trust us, we'll trick them. We'll get rid of the bears. Then you and your Mountain Men can attack and send them away."

"What?" said Jedediah Smith. "Are you crazy, Tuff? I agree Chief Black Bear will take you into his gang. He always needs more members. But those grizzlies will think you and Sadie would make a delicious snack."

"Tuff isn't afraid of the grizzlies," said Sadie. "Neither am I."

Tuff didn't look at Sadie. She might not be scared of those bears but he sure was.

"OK, then, it's a good plan. It's almost nightfall," said Jedediah. "Let's have supper. You two can sneak out of camp at first light tomorrow. Do you want us to help with your disguises?"

"Sure," said Tuff. "I guess we should make up our faces with paint."

"You're right," said Broken Hand. "We'll get the face paint ready now. We make it out of buffalo poop."

"What the –?" said Tuff. "You're going to smear buffalo poop all over our faces? Yikes."

"EEW!" cried Sadie. "That's yucky."

Broken Hand laughed. "Don't worry. Grizzly bears don't like the smell of buffalo dung either. The poop paint will keep the grizzlies away from you, at least until you have time to get rid of them."

"By the way, Tuff," said Jedediah. "Just how do you plan on getting rid of those bears?"

"Let me worry about the grizzlies," Tuff said quietly. He must think of something. He didn't want to be bear food.

CHAPTER SEVEN

DISGUISED AS SIOUX OUTLAWS

Tuff and Sadie finished their supper of buffalo sausages and quail eggs then unrolled their bedrolls.

"The sausages and eggs tasted great, didn't they, Sadie?" Tuff said.

"Um, yeah, kind of, maybe," Sadie mumbled.

Jedediah Smith came out of his tent, carrying two headdresses and Indian outfits.

"Here you go," he said. "These headdresses

are made out of golden eagle feathers. They have the Sioux Tribe colors. Try 'em on."

The Mountain Men had made up face paint out of buffalo poop then slopped it all over Tuff and Sadie's faces and arms. They put on the headdresses and changed into the Indian outfits.

"We stink," Tuff said. "But at least we have good disguises. Thanks, Jedediah."

"Good luck, Tuff. Good luck, Sadie," said Jedediah as he retreated into his tent.

"Tuff, you look worried," said Sadie.

"I am worried," Tuff said. "Judge June said we only had to chase away the outlaws, remember? She said we *might* have to worry about grizzly bears. Now we find out the outlaws have grizzlies as pets."

"Yeah. Plus, the giant Jedediah and his Mountain Men are all scared of grizzlies," said Sadie. "We're really on our own."

"Also Judge June said it's easier to *stay* out of trouble than to *get* out of trouble but we're going right into the outlaw camp," Tuff said.

The growls of a mountain lion cut through the darkness. "He sounds scary," Sadie said.

"Let's try to get some rest," Tuff said.

At first light Tuff heard the voice of a mockingbird singing the song of a blue jay. Mockingbirds got their name because they are able to copy, or "mock", the songs of other birds.

The mockingbirds are just like us, thought Tuff. *Pretending to be something they're not.* Tuff loved mockingbirds. They reminded him of Texas.

"Sadie, get up," Tuff whispered. "It's time to meet Chief Black Bear."

Tuff and Sadie loaded their saddlebags on to Silver Heels and Jenny then hopped on to the horses. They left their saddles behind.

"Indians always ride bareback," Tuff said. "So no saddles."

"Let's ride straight out into the forest," Sadie said. "Judge June said Jedediah and his men were pinned down in their camp. The Black Arrow Gang can't be far away."

"They might smell us before they see us," Tuff said. "This face paint stinks."

He saw Silver Heels' ears prick up. *I wonder?*

"THWACK!" A black arrow shot right in front of Tuff's face and landed in the tree behind him.

"THWACK!" It was followed by another.

"Get down, Sadie," Tuff cried.

"Why are they shooting arrows at us?" Sadie said. "We're Sioux Tribe, just like them."

"No, you're not," growled a voice behind them.

Tuff felt goosebumps on his arms. He and Sadie turned around.

"Sioux don't carry bullwhips," said Chief Black Bear. He nocked another arrow from his quiver and pointed it at Tuff.

Oh dear. I should have thought of that. Tuff looked around as the rest of the Black Arrow Gang appeared from behind trees. *At least I can't see any bears.*

"You come with us," Chief Black Bear said as his gang surrounded them. He rode ahead and Tuff and Sadie followed close behind on Silver Heels and Jenny.

They soon arrived at a campsite beside a roaring stream.

Tuff's heart sank. Standing in the middle of the stream, their fierce red eyes staring at Tuff and Sadie, were two enormous grizzly bears.

"I see you noticed my pets," snarled Chief Black Bear. "They're hungry. It's almost winter when they'll hibernate. Right now they're eating fish from the stream. Before too long maybe they'll be eating you."

He and his gang roared with laughter.

"Listen, Chief Black Bear," said Tuff. He'd had an idea. "We are Sioux Tribe outlaws, just like you. We're from Texas. Our tribal

leader, Chief Junia Beak, sent us here. The
bullwhips are our secret weapons. Trust us.
We'll help you get all the beaver-fur pelts you
can carry."

"You're wearing the right headdresses,"
said Chief Black Bear. "And I can smell the
same buffalo-poop paint we use. You're only

kids but maybe I'll let you join our gang. Just don't try any funny stuff. My pet grizzlies can eat you in one bite."

"Don't worry, we won't," said Sadie.

I bet they can, Tuff thought.

CHAPTER EIGHT

TUFF WARNS THE MOUNTAIN MEN

"What are you called by your tribe?" Chief Black Bear asked as he lit up a pipe. "Give us your names."

"I'm called Tuff, and this is Sadie."

"You've got some fine horses, too. They look like Comanche horses. Are they fast?" said Chief Black Bear.

"Faster than the tornado wind," said Tuff as he glanced at Sadie. "We got them from a Comanche chief."

"Then you must be very brave. You can join our gang. Here's our plan," Chief Black Bear said. "Tonight, while Jedediah Smith and his Mountain Men are sleeping, we'll surround their campsite. Then, at dawn tomorrow, we'll attack. Our two new friends from Texas, Tuff and Sadie, can use their secret-weapon bullwhips to capture Jedediah Smith's guns."

"Wait," said Tuff. "I might have a better idea. Why don't we all get on the far side of their camp, then attack from there? They'll run out toward this camp, right into the river."

"I like the way you're thinking, Tuff," said Chief Black Bear. "They'll run straight into the teeth and claws of the grizzlies."

"Ha, ha," laughed the Black Arrow Gang. "Those bears will be ready for a nice breakfast of giant Mountain Men. YUMMY."

"Hey," said Chief Black Bear to his gang. "Chase those bears out of the river so they'll stop eating. Without food all night, they'll be good and hungry in the morning."

The Black Arrow Gang moved over to the river, whooping at the bears. The two grizzlies stopped swallowing fish and rumbled over to the riverbank.

"C'mon," said Chief Black Bear, "let's have a supper of wolf sausages and hawk eggs. Tomorrow morning, we'll need all our strength to carry a full load of beaver furs. We'll be rich when we sell those pelts."

After supper, as the Black Arrow Gang fell asleep around them, Tuff and Sadie lay down near the campfire. "We've got to get to Jedediah Smith to warn him about the attack tomorrow morning," Tuff whispered. "I'm going to creep over there now."

"Now? Chief Black Bear and the gang might see you," said Sadie.

"No, they won't," whispered Tuff. "Listen to those snores. They ate so much for supper, they're like Deputy Dan. Only an explosion could wake them up."

Sadie giggled. "You're right. Those snores sound like a thunderstorm. Be careful. I'll wait for you here."

Tuff snuck over to Silver Heels and walked him silently out of the Black Arrow Gang camp. He hopped up on his horse and galloped over to Jedediah Smith's campsite.

Jedediah was outside his tent, sitting with Broken Hand beside the campfire.

"Jedediah," said Tuff as he rode up and dismounted. "Chief Black Bear is planning to attack in the morning. They're going to roar in from the far side of your camp and push you toward the river, where the grizzlies will be waiting. Chief Black Bear is not letting them eat tonight. They'll be starving."

"What are we going to do?" said Jedediah Smith. "I can fight those outlaws but I'm terrified of the grizzlies."

"I have an idea," Tuff said quietly. "Sit close and I'll whisper it to you."

Tuff whispered his idea to Jedediah and Broken Hand. They both smiled.

"I think your idea will work," said Jedediah. "We'll get ready right now."

Tuff jumped back on Silver Heels and raced across to the outlaw camp. He dismounted then crawled up to Sadie's bedroll.

Sadie was gone. *Oh no!* Tuff looked around and straight into the angry eyes of Chief Black Bear.

"Why don't you tell me where you've been, Tuff," growled Chief Black Bear, as he held his tomahawk above Sadie's head. "Drop your bullwhip next to you. Speak nice and slowly. If you don't do what I say, your ponytailed-sidekick's going to be a midnight snack for two hungry grizzly bears."

Oh dear, worried Tuff. *What can I do? Be brave.*

"One other thing," said Chief Black Bear. "All of the Sioux Tribes live in Wyoming. There aren't any Sioux in Texas. I knew that but I let you in the gang anyway. Now I want to know who you really are."

CHAPTER NINE

OUTLAW ATTACK ON JEDEDIAH SMITH'S CAMP

Tuff dropped his bullwhip to his feet. The other outlaws, with arrows loaded in their bows, surrounded him and Sadie.

"Our real names are Sheriff Tuff Brunson and Deputy Sadie Marcus," Tuff said. "Judge Junia Beak sent us here from Muleshoe, Texas. We're here to help Jedediah Smith complete his expedition to the Bighorn River. We don't like outlaw gangs one bit. Especially yours."

"Oh you don't, do you?" hollered Chief Black Bear. "I knew it. I was suspicious of you all along. Two of my gang had their bows whipped out of their hands yesterday. It was you who did it. Now the only thing I have to decide is whether to feed you to the grizzlies now or after they've eaten Jedediah Smith. What do you think, Black Arrow Gang? Now or later?"

Tuff heard the hungry bears growling from the edge of the camp.

"NOW! NOW! NOW!" the Black Arrow Gang shouted.

"It's decided then," said Chief Black Bear. "Any last words before you're munched up?"

"Yep, I've got some last words. I'm glad you won't be capturing Jedediah Smith," Tuff said as he thought how awful it would be to be eaten by a grizzly. "Because tonight I snuck over to his camp and warned him to ride out before morning. I bet he's long gone already. He's got all his beaver pelts as well. You won't get any, you ugly outlaw."

"What?" shouted Chief Black Bear. "You rascally sheriff."

"Crime doesn't pay," said Sadie.

"Here's what we'll do," Chief Black Bear said to his gang. "Use their bullwhips to tie these two kids up real tight. Dawn is breaking. Let's attack Jedediah Smith's camp right now. He might still be there." Chief Black Bear glared at Tuff and Sadie. "I'll deal with you as soon as I get back," he said with a vicious growl.

The Black Arrow Gang tied up Tuff and Sadie, then mounted their horses and rode off toward Jedediah Smith's camp.

"Quick," Tuff said to Sadie. "Let's call Silver Heels and Jenny over." They whistled to the two horses, who stood nearby at the edge of the camp.

"Is there sugar water on those whips?" Jenny neighed. "Yummy."

In just a few seconds, both horses had trotted over and stretched their heads down. They used their mouths to untie the bullwhips from around the Deputies' wrists.

"I'm so glad you remembered," said Tuff.

"Me too," said Sadie with a grin. "I always cover the bullwhips with sugar water at night. It keeps the whips loose. The horses love to come lick the sugar water off."

"That was dee-lish," Silver Heels whinnied.

"Let's get these disguises off," Tuff said as he and Sadie scraped the poop paint off their skin. "I hope Jedediah was ready for the attack. I didn't have time to tell you but I gave Jedediah and Broken Hand a good idea. Chief Black Bear should be in for a big surprise. Let's get over to Jedediah's camp."

Tuff and Sadie grabbed their saddlebags and jumped up on Silver Heels and Jenny. The horses fairly flew toward Jedediah Smith's campsite. They arrived at its outskirts just as Chief Black Bear led the Black Arrow

Gang into the camp, tomahawks held high.

"Look Sadie," Tuff said as they stopped on a small hill outside Jedediah Smith's campsite. "Notice anything different?"

Sadie looked where he was pointing. A giant Indian towered in front of a tent in the middle of the camp. The giant wore the headdress of the Sioux Tribe, as did everyone else in the camp. Sioux warpaint was smeared on their faces and arms.

Chief Black Bear and the Black Arrow Gang stopped in their tracks as they got into the middle of the camp.

"What's going on?" shouted Chief Black Bear. "Have we come to the wrong camp? This one is full of Sioux Tribe Indians."

"Hey," roared the giant Sioux. "It's Chief Black Bear and his gang. What are you filthy outlaws doing in our camp? Drop your tomahawks right now. We're taking you back to our Sioux Tribe Chief. You're under arrest."

"Do as he says," ordered Chief Black Bear

to his gang, as he lowered his tomahawk. "We've been caught by our own tribe."

Jedediah's disguised Mountain Men quickly surrounded the gang.

Tuff and Sadie lightly spurred their horses and trotted into the camp just as Chief Black Bear and the Black Arrow Gang were tied up and thrown in the prison wagon.

"Hi, Tuff," smiled Jedediah Smith as he took off his Sioux-Indian disguise and pointed at Chief Black Bear. "Look what we caught this morning. A little weaselly black bear and his cubs. Boo hoo. You had a great idea."

"You double-crossers," shouted Chief Black Bear. "I'll get you back Jedediah."

"Hey, Jedediah," smiled Tuff. "Do you think those two grizzlies are hungry? Let's go back to the Black Arrow Gang camp and find them. I bet they'd like a tasty bite of outlaw."

Jedediah didn't laugh. He'd turned as white as a ghost.

"Look behind you," Jedediah gasped.

Tuff turned around.

He was eyeball to eyeball with two giant grizzlies.

CHAPTER TEN

GRIZZLIES

"Ha, ha, I see my pets have arrived," yelled Chief Black Bear from inside the prison wagon. "Welcome, Master Bruins."

Tuff stared straight into the eyes of the biggest grizzly. He didn't want the fierce bear to think he was afraid.

Remember, Judge June had taught him, *if you meet a bear in the wild, do not run away. Speak to the bear in a strong voice.*

"Get away from me, Mr. Bear," Tuff said firmly.

"Let's slowly back the horses away," he whispered to Sadie, while still staring at the grizzly. "Jedediah Smith and his Mountain Men should be safe because they're wearing the buffalo-poop warpaint. The bears don't like the smell. But we're not. It wasn't very smart of me to suggest we take it off."

"Don't worry," said Sadie, "our horses can easily outrun these grizzlies."

"I know," said Tuff, "but our job is to get Jedediah Smith safely on his way to finish the expedition. We can't let Judge June down."

"Yee haw," yelled Chief Black Bear. "Here, grizzlies! I've got a little present for you."

Tuff watched as the two grizzlies ambled past him over to Chief Black Bear in the prison wagon.

Chief Black Bear reached in his pocket and took out two dead moles. He fed them to the bears.

"Yuk," Sadie said.

"See, these bears are harmless with me,"

Chief Black Bear said. "Now if you kids would let me and my gang out of this prison wagon, I'll take these bears with me and we'll just move right on out of here."

Chief Black Bear gave a hand signal to the grizzlies. "If you don't let us out," he snapped, "we'll sic the bears on you."

Tuff looked over at Jedediah Smith. He had never seen a giant look so scared.

"I think," said Chief Black Bear, "the wimpy little Jedediah Smith is probably so scared of these bears he's going to fall over. Aren't you, you little pile of blubbery Mountain Man?"

"What did you just call me?" said Jedediah Smith in a harsh voice.

"I called you a wimpy little pile of blubber," said Chief Black Bear.

"Uh oh," said Tuff to Sadie. "Watch out for Jedediah."

Jedediah Smith charged the prison wagon. "Nobody calls me a wimpy little pile of blubber and gets away with it," he hollered.

"Jedediah, be careful," Tuff yelled. "The grizzlies."

Tuff watched in horror as both bears stood up on their hind legs and stretched out their arms. Their sharp claws and teeth glistened in the morning sun and Jedediah stopped in his tracks.

"ROAR!" came the sound of three thousand pounds of grizzly bad mood.

I've got to do something, Tuff thought. *This better work.*

"Look out you dirty outlaw grizzly bear. Here comes Sheriff Tuff Brunson!" he cried.

He shut his eyes and cracked his whip.

"CRACK!"

He opened his eyes again and saw it had shot out and wound around the neck of the biggest bear. *Phew – that was lucky.* The bear collapsed to the ground as Tuff tightened the whip.

"CRACK!"

"I've got the other one," Sadie cried as her bullwhip wrapped around the neck of the second grizzly.

With the bullwhips tight around their necks, both grizzlies lay down quietly.

"They look like little bear cubbies." Tuff smiled at Sadie.

"Nice whip work, Deputies," Broken Hand said. "Can you show me how you use your whips? It's magical."

"Maybe," said Tuff as he winked at Sadie. He had no idea how his worked.

Tuff looked over at the prison wagon. Jedediah now had his giant hands wrapped around Chief Black Bear's neck.

"Whoa, Jedediah," Tuff said. "Hey, isn't The Rendezvous about to start? When all the Mountain Men, trappers and explorers gather to play games and swap stories?"

"It sure is," answered Jedediah. "Should we head over Appleseed Hill to The Rendezvous meeting point? It's just a mile away from here. Let's leave our camp as it is but take the prison wagon and the bears – maybe we can have some fun with these outlaws."

All the Mountain Men cheered.

"Sure," said Tuff. "Sadie and I can't stay long though. Since our job is over, we need to get back to Texas."

CHAPTER ELEVEN

THE RENDEZVOUS

"Tie those grizzlies behind the prison wagon," Jedediah Smith ordered.

"Look what I've got here," said Sadie, as she pulled the jars of honey from her saddlebags.

"Great idea, Sadie," said Jedediah, opening the jars and giving them to the grizzlies. "Bears love honey. It should keep them happy. Maybe when the jars run out they'll have a little nibble of outlaw."

The Mountain Men all roared with

laughter as they carefully tied the honey-licking bears behind the wagon.

"Here you go," said Broken Hand as he handed their whips back to Tuff and Sadie. "When you get back to Texas, please send me a magic whip."

"Those honey jars came in handy." Tuff smiled at Sadie. "But you still shouldn't have taken them from Toothless Tom."

"Oh be quiet, Tuff," said Sadie and they joined Jedediah Smith at the front of the prison wagon.

The Mountain Men followed behind the bears and they all took the trail over Appleseed Hill.

They soon reached The Rendezvous.

Jedediah hopped off his horse and gathered his friends around.

"C'mere Tuff and Sadie and meet all of my buddies," Jedediah said, pointing to each of the Mountain Men in turn. "This is 'Old Bill' Williams, 'Pegleg' Tom Smith, 'Blackfoot'

John Smith, 'Bear' Moore and 'Liver-Eating' Johnson."

"Liver?" Sadie said. "Yuk! I hate eating liver."

"I think Liver-Eating Johnson cooks it pretty good," laughed Jedediah.

"But the thought of eating liver cooked over buffalo poop? YUK!" Sadie said with disgust.

"Listen up, friends," Jedediah said to the Mountain Men. "These two law officers, Sheriff Tuff Brunson and Deputy Sadie Marcus, traveled all the way from Texas. They helped us fight off Chief Black Bear and the Black Arrow Gang. Let's make sure they have a good time at The Rendezvous."

"You bet," hollered Pegleg Tom Smith. All of Jedediah's friends clapped and shouted, "Welcome to The Rendezvous."

Tuff and Sadie grinned and doffed their hats.

"What would you kids like to eat?"

"Would you happen to have s'mores and

sarsaparilla?" Sadie asked timidly.

"S'mores and sarsaparilla?" roared Jedediah. "We've got buckets of s'mores and barrels of sarsaparilla. Roll 'em out boys."

Old Bill Williams poured Tuff and Sadie a sarsaparilla while Blackfoot John Moore handed round the s'mores.

"Hey, Tuff," said Broken Hand, between bites of a s'more. "What game would you like to play?"

"How about 'Shoot an apple off his head'?" Tuff suggested. "Maybe you can use a bow and arrow. Sound like fun?"

"Woo hoo," hollered Jedediah. "Let's all take turns shooting an apple off Chief Black Bear's head. You go first Broken Hand. I might even try shooting an arrow blindfolded."

Everybody at The Rendezvous laughed so hard they cried.

Tuff glanced over at Chief Black Bear. He wasn't laughing. He looked terrified.

"I think we ought to be going," Tuff

whispered to Sadie. They walked quietly away with Silver Heels and Jenny.

"Do you remember how to get back to The Cave?" asked Sadie.

"I do," Silver Heels whinnied. "Let's breeze back past Jedediah's camp then it's through the dark green forest." They took off at a fast gallop, rounded Jedediah's camp and, after a short ride through the forest, Silver Heels slowed as they rode into a clearing.

Tuff pulled up the reins and they stopped in front of a familiar giant saguaro cactus.

"Howdy, Tuff," said Spiky the Cactus. "Nice work. I don't like grizzlies. They always stop and pee on my legs. Who's your friend?"

"What the –?" said Tuff as he turned and looked behind him.

Sitting in Tuff's saddlebags was a beaver.

"Hello. I hopped in here back in Jedediah's camp," said the beaver. "Do you mind if I come with you? I don't want to be turned into a hat."

"I don't know," said Tuff. "What do you think, Sadie?"

"He seems nice enough," Sadie said, smiling at the beaver. "What's your name?"

"Mr. Zip," the beaver said.

"Hang on, Tuff," Spiky said. "Judge June didn't mention anything about beavers. I don't like surprises."

"It's OK, Spiky. I'll be responsible for him."

"OK. What's the password?"

"Jedediah."

"Enter."

Tuff, Sadie and Mr. Zip rode into The Cave. It was pitch black. Not a sound could be heard.

"Alright then," said Tuff. "Let's go."

Tuff and Sadie closed their eyes as a low rumble came through The Cave. They felt a cool breeze.

After the rumble stopped, they rode out into the bright Texas sunshine. Tuff smelled the spring wildflowers, the bluebonnets and

Indian paintbrushes. He loved the scent of the wildflowers.

"It's good to be home." He smiled at Sadie.

"It sure is," said Sadie. "Look, there's Judge June."

Judge June was outside The Cave entrance on Rowdy, her Paint Horse. Wild Thing peeked out of her saddlebags.

"Welcome home," Judge June said proudly. "Here's a golden star for your belt, Tuff. Good job rounding up Chief Black Bear. Not too much trouble, I hope?"

"Only a little bit," Tuff said. "We learned a lot about the Mountain Men. It's good to smell Texas wildflowers instead of Wyoming buffalo poop."

Sadie said, "We had to smear buffalo poop on our faces to disguise ourselves as Sioux outlaws."

"You can fill me in on the details." Judge June smiled as if she knew that already. "I see you brought a beaver with you. Welcome, Mr. Zip."

"Hey, how did you know his name?" Sadie asked.

"I told her," Wild Thing growled. "You're not welcome here Mr. Blip. I hate beavers. There's only room for one pet in this town. Me."

"Stop it, Wild Thing," Judge June ordered, looking down at the pink fairy armadillo. "Mr. Zip can stay here as Tuff's pet. You'll have to get along."

"Thanks, Judge June. I'm sure Wild Thing and I will be the best of friends," Mr. Zip said with a toothy smile.

Judge June looked back at Tuff and Sadie. "Should we go get a s'more and a sarsaparilla, or did you have enough at The Rendezvous?"

"Let's head for the Happy Days Saloon, Judge June," Tuff said. "We always have room for s'more s'mores."

THE END

Author's Note

The Hideout Kids series of books feature several of the same characters, animals, places and things. Here are some brief descriptions:

Charlie "Sir" Ringo: A cowboy detective.

Deputy Joe "Sawbones" Newton: Muleshoe's doctor, a deputy to Sheriff Tuff Brunson.

Deputy Sadie Marcus: Ten-year-old deputy of Muleshoe and Tuff's best friend.

Deputies: A slang term for law enforcers, including sheriffs.

Hooter: Judge June's familiar. An owl-shaped spirit who helps Judge June practice her magic.

Jelly Roll Jim, Toothless Tom, Deputy Dan Pigeon: Teenagers who grew up in Muleshoe and stayed on to help Judge June and the hideout kids.

Jenny: Sadie's Horse. A gift from Chief Ten Bears of the Comanche Tribe Indians.

Judge Junia "June" Beak: United States District Judge of the West. She is also a good and powerful witch.

Miss Hannah Humblebee: A Hopi Tribe Indian girl detective.

Mr. Zip: Tuff's pet. A beaver.

Muleshoe, Texas: Home of the hideout kids. Only children can find it and live there.

S'mores: Chocolate-covered marshmallows, served on sugar crackers. Dee-lish.

Sarsaparilla: The most popular soft drink of the Wild West. It's thought to have healing powers and is made from the root of the sarsaparilla vine. Yummy.

Sheriff Tuff Brunson: Ten-year-old sheriff of Muleshoe.

Silver Heels: Tuff's horse. Also a gift from Chief Ten Bears.

Spiky: A giant saguaro cactus that guards The Cave.

The Cave: A magical place where the kids can travel through time.

The Singing Cowboy Poet: A magical elf.

Wild Thing: Judge June's pet. A pink fairy armadillo.

This book mentions some words, things and events that my readers might not have heard before. Here are some simple explanations and definitions to explain them.

Hibernate: To have a long sleep over winter, like bears do.

Sic: To attack.

MACHO NACHO
& THE COWBOY BATTLE

Chapter One
HONEYBEES

It was noon on a hot June day in the Wild West Texas town of Muleshoe.

Sheriff Tuff Brunson walked down Muleshoe's dusty main street. He felt lazy. Thousands of cicadas buzzed in the mesquite trees around the town. *What should I have for lunch today?* he wondered as he neared the Happy Days Saloon. The delicious smell of grilled beef tacos and burritos filled his nose.

"Hey, it's the tiny cowboy poet," he said to himself as he looked down the veranda of the saloon. The little poet with the short legs and big hat sat back in his rocking chair and sang,

I like to smell the corn chips
I like to hear the bees
And what I like to eat the most
Is beef tacos with peas

'Cause when I eat a taco
I also like a nacho
'cept when things go loco
And the nacho is too macho

What a funny song, Tuff thought.

"Sheriff Brunson, come quick," said a boy's voice as Tuff passed the Muleshoe jailhouse, which sat on Main Street next to the Happy Days. "We've got a big problem."

Tuff rounded the corner and looked toward the horse stables behind the jailhouse, where the voice seemed to come from. It sounded like a voice he knew.

"What the –?" Tuff said.

Outside the horse stables stood three people, dressed in white outfits. Tuff couldn't see their faces and hands, which were covered by masks and gloves.

"There's a problem in the stables," said the tallest masked person. "You need to come and see now."

Tuff didn't know who these three people in their strange outfits were but thought he had better make sure his horse Silver Heels was alright. He lowered his fingers to the bullwhip which hung from his star-studded belt and followed them as they kicked hay aside and walked into the stables.

As Tuff stepped inside, the smallest person quickly ran behind him and slammed the stable door shut. "Now," squealed a girl's voice.

Silver Heels whinnied, "Look out, Tuff."

He watched in horror as the remaining

two masked people threw a saddle blanket aside. Underneath was a giant beehive. As soon as the blanket hit the ground the swarm spread out across the stables. The terrible sound of buzzing honeybees filled the air as they swooped and dove around Tuff's head. He knew no bullwhip could help him now.

"There's nowhere to hide, you bumbling sheriff," shouted the tallest masked person, who Tuff realized now was dressed like a beekeeper. "Forty thousand honeybees will sting you. The only place you can escape is inside the jail."

Tuff knew the beekeeper was right. With his arm across his face to protect his eyes from the bees, he ran into the next building. He heard a door crash shut behind him. Tuff lowered his arm from his eyes and realized he was locked in one of his own jail cells.

The three beekeepers appeared outside the cell.

"Ha, ha," laughed the tallest as he took off his mask. "You fell for our trick."

It wasn't a beekeeper at all. Tuff stared into the nasty red eyes of "Big Nose" George Parrot, the meanest outlaw in the Wild West.

"Yeah," said the other two as they also took off their masks, gloves and white outfits. "It's 'Little Nose' George and 'Tiny Nose' Peggy, you dumb sheriff."

"We've got the sheriff locked in his own jail," said Big Nose George. "Now let's go have a delicious lunch at the Happy Days Saloon. After lunch we'll help ourselves to all the hideout kids' tooth fairy money."

"Then, for dessert, we'll come back and have big bowls of honey," said Tiny Nose Peggy.

"If you rob the kids, you're the ones who will get stung," said Tuff.

"Oh, so should we 'bee' careful?" said Big Nose George.

"Ha, ha, ha!" laughed The Parrot Gang as the three outlaws danced out of the jailhouse, slamming the door behind them.

So far in the HIDEOUT KIDS series...

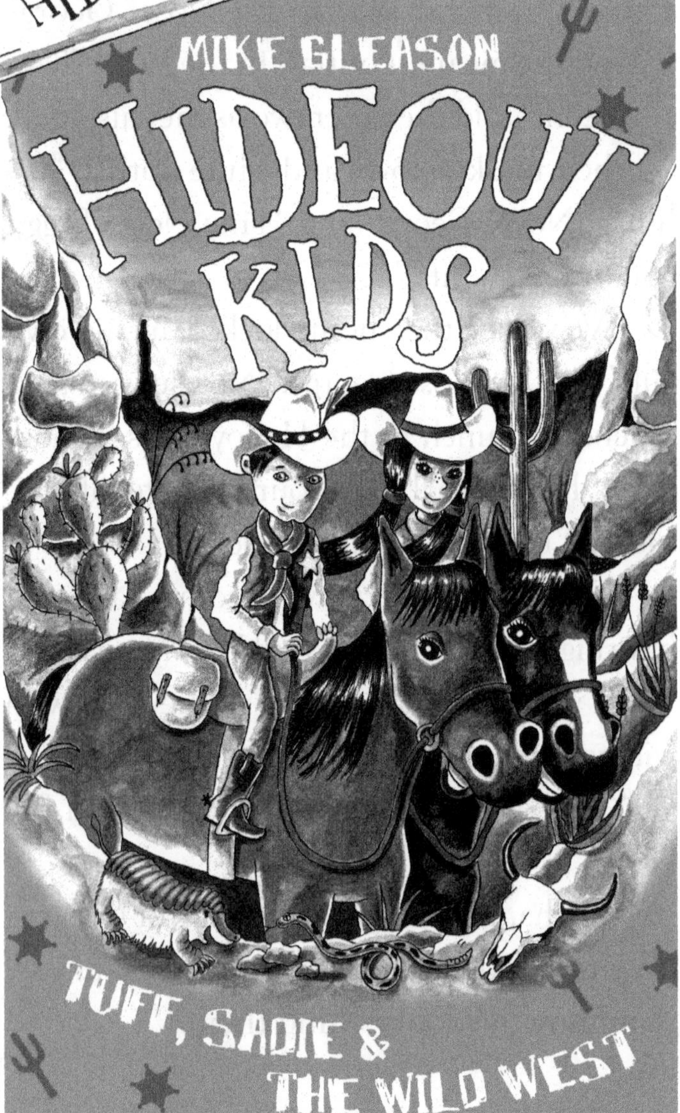

MIKE GLEASON

HIDEOUT KIDS

GENERAL MUSTER &
NO-TREES TOWN

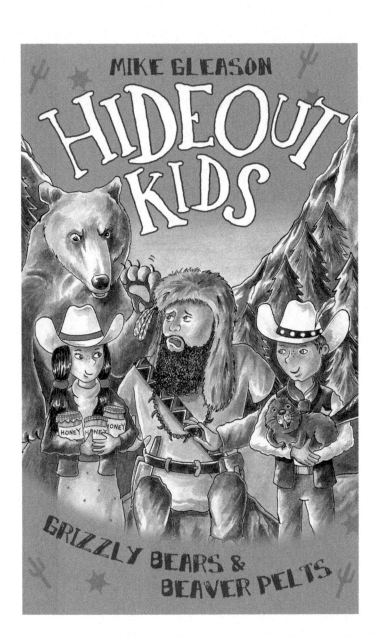

ABOUT THE AUTHOR

Hideout Kids author Mike Gleason comes from a small town in Texas. He grew up with cowboys, cowgirls and exciting stories of Wild West adventures. He was a wildcatter in the Texas oil fields and a board director at MGM in Hollywood. He created and produced an award-winning music television series at Abbey Road Studios. He lives and writes in London.

ABOUT THE ILLUSTRATOR

Hideout Kids illustrator Victoria Taylor comes from Cheltenham, England, and her love of art was inspired by her maternal grandmother. She trained at Plymouth University and worked for many years as a graphic designer. Having returned to her first love of painting and drawing, Victoria is now a freelance book illustrator. She lives in Gloucestershire with her husband and two children.